Hey, Little Ant

Hey, Little Ant

Phillip and Hannah Hoose

Illustrations by Debbie Tilley

SCHOLASTIC INC.
New York Toronto London Auckland Sydney
Mexico City New Delhi Hong Kong

KID: Hey, little ant down in the crack,

Can you hear me? Can you talk back?

See my shoe, can you see that?

Well, now it's gonna **squish** you flat!

WIST OFF

ANT: Please, oh please, do not squish me,

Change your mind and let me be,

I'm on my way with a crumb of pie,

Please, oh **please**, don't make me die!

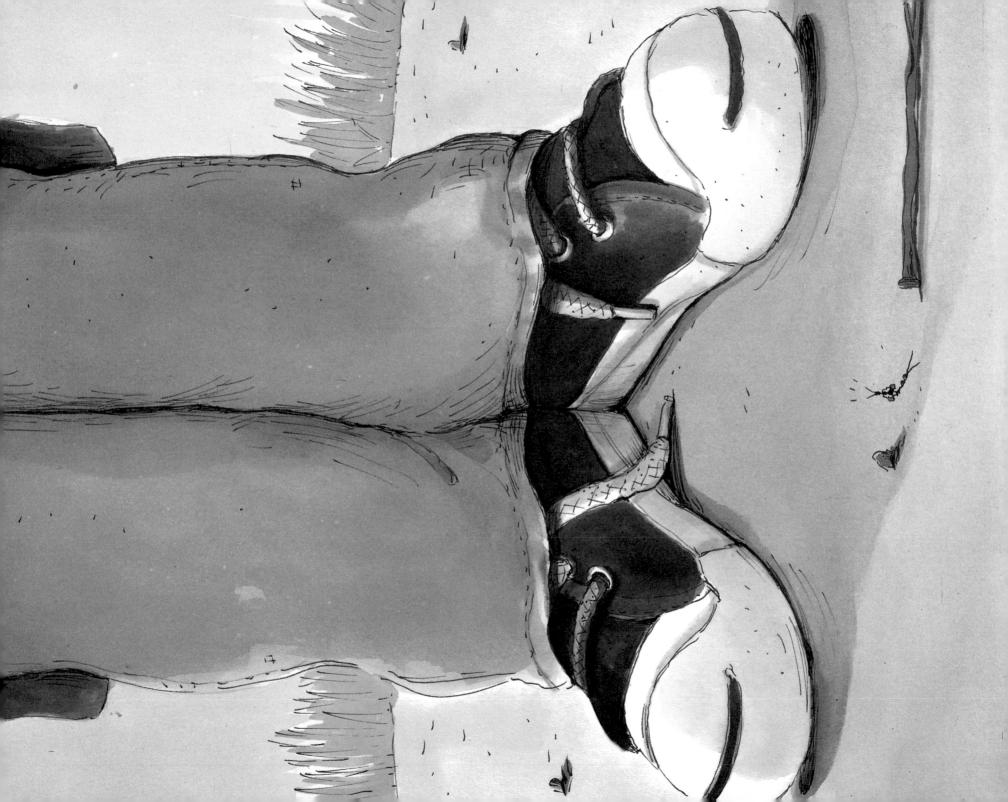

ANT: But you are a giant and giants can't
know how it feels to be an ant.
Come down close, I think you'll see
That you are very much like me.

KID: Are you crazy? **Me** like **you**?

I have a home and a family, too.

You're just a speck that runs around,
No one would care if my foot came down.

KID: But my mom says that ants are rude,

They carry off our picnic food!

They steal our chips and bread crumbs, too,

It's **good** if I squish a crook like you.

ANT: Hey, I'm not a crook, kid, read my lips!

Sometimes ants need crumbs and chips.

One little chip can feed my town,

So please don't make your shoe come down.

KID: But all my friends squish ants each day,
Squishing ants is a game we play.

YEAH

They're looking at me—they're listening, too.
They all say I **should** squish you.

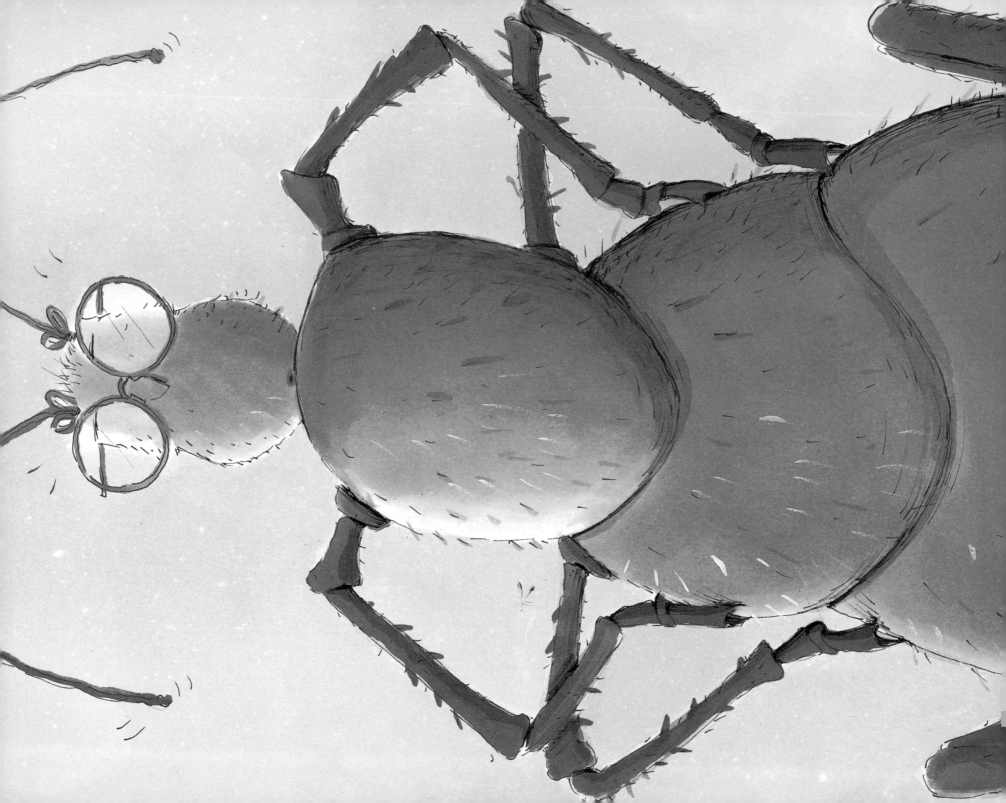

ANT: I can see you're big and strong,

Decide for yourself what's

right and wrong,

If you were me and I were you,

What would **you** want **me** to do?

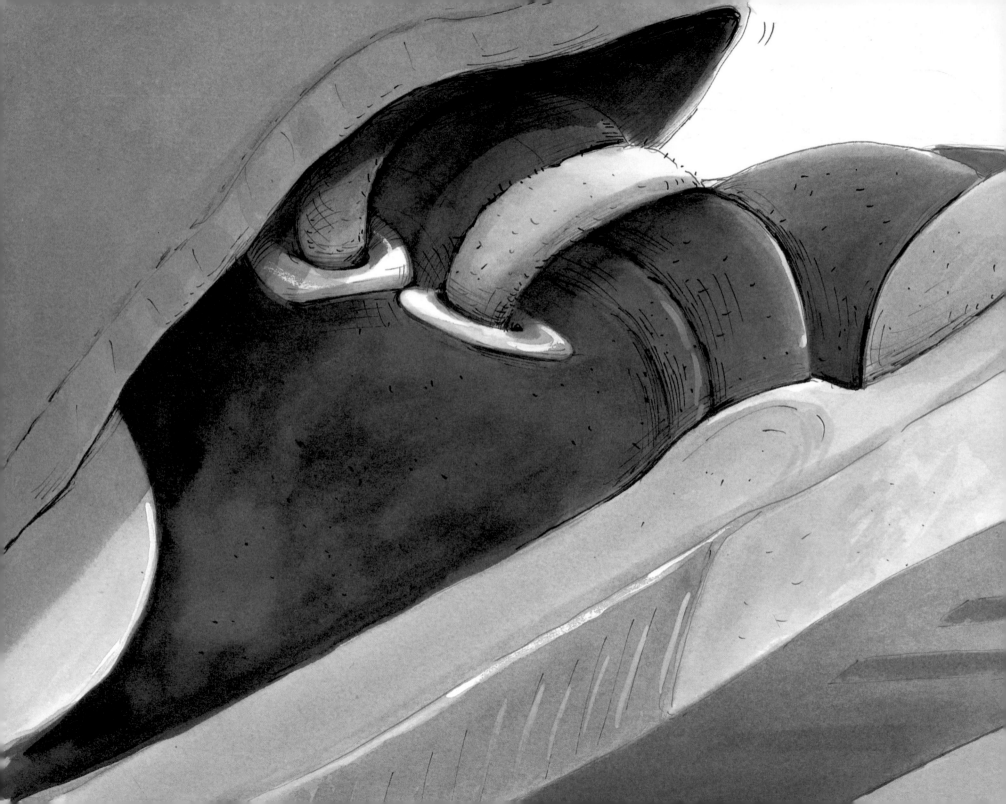

Should the ant get squished? Should the ant go free?

It's up to the kid, not up to me.

We'll leave the kid with the raised-up shoe.

What do you think that kid should do?

1. **KID:** Hey, little ant down in the crack,
Can you hear me? Can you talk back?
See my shoe, can you see that?
Well now it's gonna **squish** you flat!

2. **ANT:** Please, oh please, do not squish me,
Change your mind and let me be,
I'm on my way with a crumb of pie,
Please, oh **please,** don't make me die!

3. **KID:** Anyone knows that ants can't feel.
You're so tiny you don't look real.
I'm so big and you're so small,
I don't think it'll hurt at all.

4. **ANT:** But you are a giant and giants can't
Know how it feels to be an ant.
Come down close, I think you'll see
That you are very much like me.

5. **KID:** Are you crazy? **Me** like **you**?
I have a home and a family, too.
You're just a speck that runs around,
No one would care if my foot came down.

6. **ANT:** Oh big friend, you are so wrong,
My nest mates need me 'cause I am strong.
I dig our nest and feed baby ants, too,
I must not die beneath your shoe.

7. **KID:** But my mom says that ants are rude,
They carry off our picnic food!
They steal our chips and bread crumbs, too,
It's **good** if I squish a crook like you.

8. **ANT:** Hey, I'm not a crook, kid, read my lips!
Sometimes ants need crumbs and chips.
One little chip can feed my town,
So please don't make your shoe come down.

9. **KID:** But all my friends squish ants each day,
Squishing ants is a game we play.
They're looking at me—they're listening, too.
They all say I **should** squish you.

10. **ANT:** I can see you're big and strong,
Decide for yourself what's right and wrong,
If you were me and I were you,
What would **you** want **me** to do?

11. Should the ant get squished? Should the ant go free?
It's up to the kid, not up to me.
We'll leave the kid with the raised-up shoe.
What do you think that kid should do?

To all squished ants. -**H.H.**

To Ruby with the raised-up shoe. -**P.H.**

To Ian and his family, with special thanks
to Eric for his Hey, Little Centipede idea. -**D.T.**

ISBN 0-439-08565-9

Text copyright © 1998 by Phillip and Hannah Hoose.
Illustrations copyright © 1998 by Debbie Tilley.
Music copyright © 1992 by Precious Pie Music, Inc., BMI.
All rights reserved. Published by Scholastic Inc.,
555 Broadway, New York, NY 10012, by arrangement
with Tricycle Press. SCHOLASTIC
and associated logos are trademarks and/or
registered trademarks of Scholastic Inc.

12 11 10 9 8 7 6 5 4   0 1 2 3 4/0

Printed in the U.S.A.   08

First Scholastic printing, September 1999
Book design by Susan Van Horn